MW00580799

" Dance ï Sing with me ! "

Love
Lisa Cappelli

This Book Belongs To:

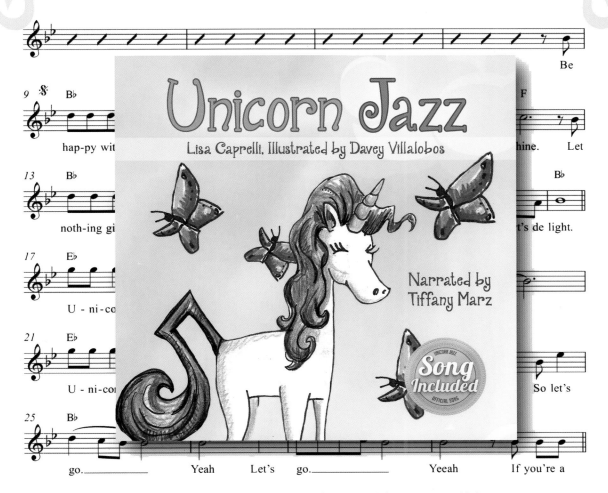

You can hear this story come to life on Audible and Amazon Prime Video.
In addition, the "Unicorn Jazz Friendship Song" that accompanies the lyrics
in this book can be found on Itunes, Spotify, YouTube Music, Iheart Radio,
Amazon Music and more music platforms.   Go to: UnicornJazz.com

Copyright 2018

All rights reserved

ISBN: 978-1-64516-798-3

Library of Congress Number 2019910012

Published by Happy Lifestyle Online

All rights reserved. No part of this book may be reproduced or transmitted in
any form or by any means, electronic or mechanical, including photocopying,
recording or by an information storage and retrieval system - except by a
reviewer who may quote brief passages in a review to be printed in a magazine
or blog - with permission in writing from the author.

Unicorn Jazz

Lisa Caprelli, Author

Davey Villalobos, Illustrator

Dedication by the Author:

Inspired by my beautiful niece, Jasmine, who always has a positive outlook in life
and always sees the best in others.

May you never take a single day fora granted!

And for all you unicorn lovers, never stop believing.

Dedication by the Illustrator:

For my girls, Avery and Eleya ... all my love.

Once there was a unicorn named Jazz.
She was kind, friendly, and a bit shy.

She looked like a horse,
but with a golden horn
in the middle of her head.

Her father
was **Big** and
Strong.

Her mother
was **kind**
and clever.

Deep inside, Jazz wanted to be a singer.

She was amazed when her mother sang to her. Her mother's voice made her feel brave.

Although Jazz was talented like her mother, she was afraid to sing. She was too shy.

But whenever Jazz was alone, she sang out loud to herself, the same song her mother sang to her...

"Be HAPPY with your light. You are bold, you shine sooo bright, a Golden ray you're my Sunshine! Let nothing give you fright you are strong your heart is kind. And everyday you're my heart's delight..."

These words made Jazz feel brave.

One day, Jazz and her family
moved to a magical land.

Mona
the Elephant*

This land had ALL SORTS of animals.

There were birds
who sang
the sweetest tunes...

along with horses,

giraffes,

lizards and geckos!

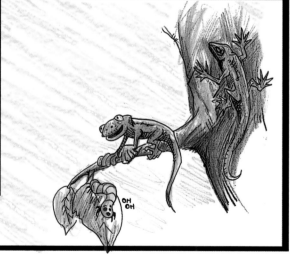

Jazz desperately wanted to make friends
with these animals but she felt like
she didn't belong.

"How am I going to fit in?
I don't think anyone
likes me here,"
she sighed.

The unicorn family
was not the same
as the other animals here.

Unicorns like to sing - a lot!

U

Unicorn... noun. (yew-knee-corn)
Magical. Like to sing a lot

Unicycle... noun (you-neh-sike-l)
clown transportation

Universe... noun. (you-nah-verse)
here there and everywhere

University...noun (you-nah-verse-a-t)
where youlearn about stuff

Whenever Jazz wanted
to make new friends, she would
sing a silly chant:

"Gonna go out,
make a friend or two,
laugh with, play with,
under skies sooo blue!"

Soon school would start, and Jazz
was afraid she would not find
friends like her.

She tried to make friends with the horses.

She did not look like a horse with
that big golden horn on her head.

"You don't look like a real horse," one said.
"Horses do NOT sing," said another.

They did not want to play with her.
The horses just stared at Jazz
and wondered what kind of horse
had a horn on her head.

Jazz walked away and tried to make friends
with the giraffes. The giraffes had
two tiny horns on their heads.

The giraffes told Jazz she was not tall like a giraffe.

They said,
"How will you
eat the tops
of the trees?
You cannot
see as high
as we can."

Jazz tried to show them that she could eat the tops
of the trees, but the trees were way too tall,
and her neck was too short.
"They are right. I'm nothing like a giraffe,"
and she sadly walked away...
Jazz was faster, more colorful, and had
just one single horn.
The animals ignored her, and Jazz
went off in search of new friends.

Soon Jazz found some lizards and geckos.
Some could change colors and blend into objects.
This made them very good at hiding.

"You are probably not very good
at hide and seek," they told her.

Jazz was not able to hide her color.
Although she tried to hide it, it was not
very fun because the gecko always found her.

Jazz told her mother she didn't
want to go to school.
"I am so different. I don't think anyone will like me."

Her mother sang:

"Be happy with your light. You are bold, you shine sooo bright,
a Golden ray you're my sunshine! Let nothing give you fright
you are strong, your heart is kind and everyday
you're my heart's delight..."

With grace, her mother said,"You should love what
makes you unique. You are adorable and can sing
better than anyone I know, Jazzy girl."

Jazz was so worried about going to school and not making any friends that she wandered into the mountains by herself.

There were no friends to play with in this new place. Jazz felt sad and alone.

Jazz wanted to feel happy, so she sang the song her mother taught her.

As she was singing, a bird flew down.

He was not like other birds.
His feathers were black and white
and not at all colorful.

In a raspy voice, he said, "Look at YOU!
You have a beautiful voice."

Jazz was surprised.
"Thank you. Who are you?"
she replied bashfully.

Only her Momma had ever said nice
things about her voice.

"My name is Woof!"

"I am a Crow. I know, you must be thinking, who would take a name like Woof seriously?"

"I have a name that a dog should have."

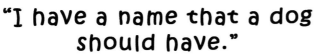

Woof continued to stare at Jazz and said, "You, my dear, are an AMAZING singer! Your voice is so, so magical. What I wouldn't give for a voice like yours!"

Stunned, she replied,
"I don't think I'm magical, really...
the other animals don't understand me,
because I look different."

"Hmm, well, you do have a lot of
beauty and color, you know?"
said Woof.

"You have a strong, glorious horn!
You sing more beautifully
than any other bird I've ever heard."

Jazz smiled ear to ear.

"The other birds
do not think I am like them," said Woof,

"But that does
not stop me from being who
I want to be. I have a great
memory, too.

Listen to me hum your song."

Instantly, Woof hummed the
exact tune that Jazz just sang
moments before.

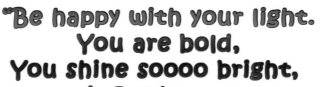

"Be happy with your light.
You are bold,
You shine soooo bright,
A Golden ray
You're my sunshine
Let nothing give you fright
You are strong
Your heart is kind.
And everyday
You're my heart's delight..."

"You are very smart, Woof!
I see what makes YOU unique now."

Jazz was happy.
She found a friend.

"You should always be proud of what
makes you special," said Woof. "I bet, if you showed
others your beautiful voice, they would agree."

"I'm not afraid to sing loud,"
and in a raspy voice, Woof sang:

"What do you do with a friend like yooo-"

They both laughed.
"Maybe you should let me sing.
That did not sound very good, but you still
had fun doing it, right?"

"Yes, of course. Now you sing," said Woof.
Boldly and loudly, Jazz sang.

The next day, Jazz bravely sang
as she entered the schoolyard.

All the animals
stopped and stared.

The lizards spoke, "You have such
beautiful colors and sing with
such grace. You can't play hide and seek,
but you can sing?"

The horses spoke. "You aren't a horse. No horse
could sing so beautifully. We are sorry,
we didn't realize how AWESOME you are!
Can you teach us how to sing like you?"

Blushing, Jazz nodded.
"Only if you let me race with you!"

Yay I Say!

They all laughed and were happy.

Jazz did not feel alone anymore.
She was not afraid to show off her talent.

All the animals asked to play games with Jazz:
Play hopscotch with me!
Color with me!
Sing with me!
Dance with me!

She was glad that she was different.
Jazz had a message in a song to share:

"Be Happy with your light.
You are bold,
You shine sooo bright,
A Golden ray
You're my sunshine!
Let nothing give you fright
You are strong
Your heart is kind.
And everyday
You're my heart's delight

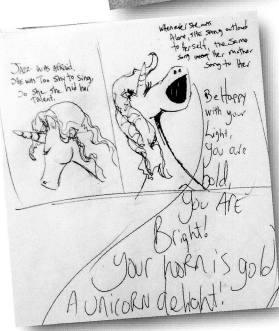

Mona The Elephant—a Cherished Zoo Animal

Mona, an Asian Elephant, was among the most popular animals to visit at the zoo. She came to **El Paso** in 1956 at 700 pounds.

The Asian elephant is the only living species of the "genus **Elephas**" and is distributed in the Indian subcontinent and Southeast Asia, from **India** and **Nepal** in the west to **Borneo** in the south.

The **El Paso Zoo** has a lot of history on its beginnings to where it is now. It is now a regional attraction featuring dynamic conservation education programs and experiences with animals from around the world.

From the Author:

"Let's go see **Mona**!" That was a common request I had as a little girl, and I got to grow up with her, as did many of her fans.

About The Author and Illustrator

Lisa Caprelli is a Latina mother who enjoys creative writing, teaching and researching to create a culture of understanding and communication sprinkled with happiness.

The Unicorn Jazz series are based on lessons and experiences she had growing up with her siblings and also that as a mother. Her books are praised for the social emotional learning, emotional intelligence with a creative flair to connect children and educators with meaningful conversations. Her inquisitive nature of understanding human behavior drew her to study and graduate with a Bachelor's of Science in Social Psychology.

Born and raised in El Paso, Texas she settled in Orange County, California in 2001.

And with a 25 year branding, public relations, FM/AM radio and podcasting background, Lisa has made writing her life. She enjoys speaking to diverse audiences of all ages, from elementary schools, teens and millennials, to adult educators such as librarians, principals, counselors and more. Lisa is proud wife to her partner, **Dr. Chris**; mother of two sons, Matthew (a nurse) and Trey (a popular YouTuber—under the name TreyJam.com

Davey Villalobos resides in El Paso, Texas. He is a proud uncle, baker by trade, avid reader and cycling enthusiast. He has been drawing since he was able to hold a crayon.

———————————————————————

Acknowledgements—This book and Unicorn Jazz's vision would not be possible without many awesome people who contributed:

Family: Jasmine Powers; my momma Hope Hernandez; Tia Lucy Dominguez; Alyssa Ruiz, Lori Vasquez, Marcello Funk; my sons: Matthew Vasquez & Trey Solomon

Siblings: Debbie Powers, Suzanne Funk, Ruth Leigh, Mike Hernandez;

Friends: Thanecha Anderson, Blake Pinto, Aisha Armer, Donna Hernandez; Luisa & Joe Dorsey, Holda Dorsey, Alexis Maron, Teri Sawyer, Michele Kennedy.

Last but not Least: My *Woof the Crow's*—these people believed in me:

Chris Herzig, Cindy Kirkland, Rg Lutz, Kanani Lutz, Miguel Barillas, Kerri Kasem, Claudia Dangerfield, Alex Agahi, Ibonne Demogines, Lizette Ruiz, Sophia Ruiz, Lakeview Times, Del Norte Elementary, and more listed on our website under "Team."

I BELIEVE IN YOU!
~Woof the Crow

More Books & Products By Unicorn Jazz™

UnicornJazz.com

Be sure to grab the next Unicorn Jazz Books in its series.

Teacher Curriculum, coloring pages, activities, resources, 3d Printer file of Unicorn Jazz, Unicorn Jazz plush, and more are available to accompany this book! Librarians/Teachers, we offer in person or Skype Author Visits for your classroom! Visit:

UnicornJazz.com /Author-Visits

If you like this book, please review on Amazon, Goodreads or Google! We thrive on positive reviews and feedback!

The End